The Worst Best Friend

by Alexis O'Neill

Illustrated by
Laura Huliska-Beith

Scholastic Press
New York

Library of Congress Cataloging-in-Publication Data:
O'Neill, Alexis, 1949–
The worst best friend / by Alexis O'Neill ; illustrated by Laura Huliska-Beith. — 1st ed.   p.   cm.
Summary: When a new boy named Victor arrives at school, Conrad temporarily forgets about his best friend Mike, but when Victor's desire to win makes him not want Conrad on his team, Mike and Conrad discover that they are still best friends after all.
ISBN-13: 978-0-545-01023-8 (hardcover : alk. paper)   ISBN-10: 0-545-01023-3 (hardcover : alk. paper)
[1. Best friends—Fiction. 2. Friendship—Fiction. 3. Schools—Fiction.] I. Huliska-Beith, Laura, 1964– ill. II. Title.
PZ7.O5523Wo 2009   [E]—dc22   2007036242

12 11 10 9 9 7 6 5 4 3 2 1   09 09 10 11 12
Printed in Singapore 46
First edition, September 2009

The display type was set in Eatwell Chubby and Drunk Robot Farmers Daughter.
The text type was set in 14-point Futura.
Book design by Marijka Kostiw

Famous
Not-so-Big
People

Napoleon
Thumbelina
Mini-Me

With thanks to the students of Baldwin Stocker School in Arcadia, California,

and with love to BBFs Barbara & Linda, Donna & Corinne, my DKB, Dot, and (always) Ede. — A.O.

And a huge *thank you* to Leslie and Marijka for helping me make the best, best art I possibly could. — L.H.B.

In memory of Tip and John
and brothers Steve and Mike Mahoney. — A.O.

For my best, BEST friend, Jeff.
(Full tilt on the Friend-o-Meter) — L.H.B.

Mike and Conrad,
Conrad and Mike

were best,
BEST
friends.

High five, high five

Knuckle, knuckle

Clap

Shoulder tap, shoulder tap

Stomp, stomp

Snap!

Mike and Conrad, Conrad and Mike

Ate together

Read together

Played together—

Kickball, basketball, dodgeball, tag.

And then one day . . .

. . . the principal popped in.

Beside him
stood a boy.
A big, **BIG** boy.
"Hello, class.
This is Victor.
He is new."

"Heyyyyy!" called Victor.
"Heyyyyy!" called the class.
"HEYYYY!"
called Conrad above them all.
"Come sit with US!"

So Mike and Conrad,

Conrad and Mike,

the best, best friends, made room for Victor

at their table.

During recess,

Victor yakked and bragged and blabbed.

"See? I have a medal for **EVERY** sport."

"Wowwww!" said Conrad.

Mike said, "Come on—let's play."

"Let's stay!" said Conrad. **"He—is—awesome!"**

Victor

yakked

and

bragged

and

blabbed

some

more.

Mike walked away.

The next day,
it was Conrad and **VICTOR, VICTOR** and Conrad.

They walked together

Ate together

Played together—

No room for Mike.

What happened to Mike's best, best friend? Just like THAT, Conrad had become the WORST best friend.

Mike could not decide—

Was he **SAD??**

Was he **MAD??**

What was he to do?

That afternoon, Mike zoomed from the room. He hit the playground

zip, zap, zup.

"Hey! Who wants to play?" Mike called, the kickball in his hand.

Victor yelled, "I'm captain of the Red Team. Who wants to **WIN?**"

Mike steamed.
That boy was new!
He took Mike's friend—
Mike's best, best friend
—and called out
"captain" *first*.

"Well,
I'm captain
of the
Blue Team,"
Mike
yelled back.

They chose up sides.

Mike picked a kid.

Then Victor picked a **BIG** kid.

Mike picked a kid.

Then Victor picked a **BIG, BIG** kid.

No one picked Conrad.

Back and forth the captains went.

"Hey, Victor,"

whispered Conrad.

"What about me?"

"Look, pal," Victor blasted.
"I want to **WIN**.

Big kids—**WOW!**

They can **POW** the ball right out of sight.

You're—not—

BIG."

Mike watched his friend — **his worst best friend** —

slump against the fence.

No fair, thought Mike.

How could Victor do that?

Then Mike said, "I choose **CONRAD.**"

"Me?" asked Conrad.

"You," said Mike. "Play ball."

The teams warmed up.

The game began.

Pitch.

Kick.

Run.

Catch.

Three times the Red Team snatched that ball.

"You're out! We're up!" yelled Victor from the field.

The Blue Team pitched and ran and jumped.

But that ball whizzed past so fast and high,

Mike's Blue Team could not reach.

And one by one, the Big Kids rammed and slammed that ball clear out of sight. Each inning was the same.

"We won! We won!"

crowed Victor

from home plate.

He danced a victory dance.

Conrad

looked

at Victor.

Conrad

looked

at Mike.

And to his friend,

his TRUE-BLUE friend,

he said,

"Thanks for picking me."

Mike tossed the ball against the wall.

"I've been the WORST best friend," said Conrad.

"The worst, WORST friend," said Mike.

Conrad hung his head. "Still friends?" he asked.

Mike bounced the ball.

He spun the ball.

He gave the ball a big kick.

"Hmmm . . ."

So Mike and Conrad,

Conrad and Mike

were

best,

BEST

friends—

again.

High five, high five

Knuckle, knuckle

Clap

Shoulder tap, shoulder tap

Stomp, stomp

Snap!